Disney's *Early Reader* books are designed for children at different levels of reading ability.

PRE-READERS

PRE-**1** LEVEL

- Picture reading
- Repetition of words
- Short, simple sentences

BEGINNING TO READ

1 LEVEL

- Rhyming text
- Expanded vocabulary
- Longer sentences

INDEPENDENT READERS

2 LEVEL

- Phonetic words
- Opposites and soundalike words
- Greater sentence variety

READING LEADERS

3 LEVEL

- Wide vocabulary
- Challenging stories
- Chapter-book format

First Edition
V381-8386-5-10064
Library of Congress Cataloging-in-Publication Data on file
ISBN 978-1-4231-2581-5

Manufactured in the USA
For more Disney Press fun, visit www.disneybooks.com

SUSTAINABLE FORESTRY INITIATIVE

Certified Chain of Custody
35% Certified Forests,
65% Certified Fiber Sourcing
www.sfiprogram.org

Clubhouse Adventures

Disney PRESS

NEW YORK

CONTENTS

Donald's Lost Lion

A LEVEL PRE-1 EARLY READER

By Susan Ring

Illustrated by Loter, Inc.

DISNEY PRESS

NEW YORK

Look! There is Mickey Mouse!
Let's play with Donald and Mickey today.
Just say Meeska, Mooska, Mickey Mouse!
Let's go in the Clubhouse.

There is Donald Duck.

Oh, no! He has lost his toy.

It is a lion named .

Sparky

He can **ROAR!**

roar

Donald can't go to sleep without him.

We must find before bedtime.

Sparky

Here is Toodles! He has come to help.

His tools can help us find .

Sparky

What tools will we use today?

We will use a , a , and a .

microphone   ladder   mask

Where could  be?
Sparky

First, Donald went to the pond.

Maybe Sparky fell into the pond.

Which tool can we use to find out?

We will use the mask .

No, Sparky did not fall into the pond.

14

15

Next, Donald went to the park.

Maybe  Sparky went up the tree.

Which tool can we use to find out?

We will use the  ladder .

No,  Sparky did not go up the tree.

16

Then, Donald went to the beach.

Look! Goofy is at the beach.

Goofy saw a lion. It had big, green eyes.

The lion made a big **ROAR!**
roar

Could  be here at the beach?

Sparky

Which tool can we use to find out?

We will use the .

microphone

Maybe we can hear him **ROAR!**

roar

Everybody listens for  .
Sparky

They hear three things.

First, they hear bees .

After that, they hear frogs .

Then, they hear a monkey !

Donald finds a monkey on the sand.

22

What do they hear next?

They hear a ROAR!

It sounds like roar . Sparky

But they don't see . Sparky

They see Pete.

Pete has 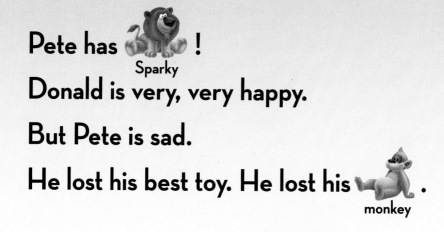 !
Sparky

Donald is very, very happy.

But Pete is sad.

He lost his best toy. He lost his monkey .

Donald gives the  to Pete.

monkey

Pete gives  to Donald.

Sparky

Now, everybody is happy.

It is time for Donald to go home.

Good night, Donald.

Good night, .

Sparky

ROAR!

Roar

30

Go, Goofy, Go!

A LEVEL PRE-1 EARLY READER

By Sheila Sweeny Higginson

Illustrated by Loter, Inc.

Goofy wants to go and play.
How will he get to the Clubhouse today?

Goofy scoots all around.
Then he crashes to the ground.

GOOF

No, Goofy, no!
Scooting is not the way to go.

Goofy flies in a plane.
Then it breaks down in the rain.

No, Goofy, no!
Flying is not the way to go.

Goofy rows in a boat.
Then he cannot stay afloat.

No, Goofy, no!
Rowing is not the way to go.

Goofy bounces on a stick.
Then he trips over a brick.

No, Goofy, no!
Bouncing is not the way to go.

Goofy glides through the air.
Then he lands next to a bear.

No, Goofy, no!
Gliding is not the way to go.

Goofy skates on a lake.
Then the ice begins to break.

No, Goofy, no!
Skating is not the way to go.

Goofy surfs on a wave.
Then he ends up in a cave.

No, Goofy, no!
Surfing is not the way to go.

Goofy slides down a line.
Then he gets tangled in a vine.

No, Goofy, no!
Sliding is not the way to go.

Goofy sails next to a whale.
Then he flips onto its tail.

No, Goofy, no!
Sailing is not the way to go.

Goofy stops to have a treat.
Then he looks down at his feet.

Goofy wonders if you know,
A new way that he can go.

Yes, Goofy, yes!
Walking is the way that's best!

The Mystery of the Missing Muffins

A Level 1 Early Reader

By Sheila Sweeny Higginson

Illustrated by Loter, Inc.

DISNEP PRESS

NEW YORK

Hello, everybody!
Do you want to come to my Clubhouse?
Well, all right. Let's go!
Just say, "Meeska, Mooska,
Mickey Mouse!"

Do you smell something baking?
It's my muffins!
I made them to share with my friends.
It's time for roll call!
Donald! Daisy! Goofy! Pluto! Minnie!

How many muffins are there?
Let's count them together:
1, 2, 3, 4, 5, 6.

Ouch! These muffins are too hot.

Oh, Toodles!
We need your help.
Let's see—a set of keys, a measuring tape,
a fan, and the Mystery Mouseketool.
Which one will cool the muffins?

Cheers! We've got ears!
A fan will do the job!
Now, just wait a minute while I turn it on.

Goofy, will you hold the muffins for me?
Thanks!

Ding-dong!
Did you hear that sound?
Let's go see who is at the door.

It's Donald!
He's been busy cleaning out his closet.
All of that work has made Donald terribly
hungry.
I bet he would like one of my tasty muffins.

Oh, no!
My muffins are missing!

Calling all clues!
We need to find my muffins right away!

Will you help me find my muffins?
Great! Donald wants to help, too.
He found the perfect detective hat.

Do you see anything we can use to find clues?
You're right! A magnifying glass will help us.

Calling all clues!
Do you see the handprint?
It means that whoever took the muffins
has hands.
Pluto, I guess you didn't take them.

Calling all clues!
Detective Donald has found a trail of crumbs.
It leads to a small door.

We need a tool to help us measure the suspects' heights.
Should we use the set of keys, the measuring tape, or the Mystery Mouseketool?

The measuring tape will do the job!
Goofy, you are too big to fit through the door.
You didn't take the muffins.

Calling all clues!
Donald sees a wooden box and a big
mud puddle at the end of the trail.
But where are my muffins?

Let's turn around and go back inside.
Yikes! The Clubhouse door is locked.
Which Mouseketool should we use to unlock
the door—the set of keys or the Mystery
Mouseketool?

Did you say the set of keys?
You're right!
Now find the key that matches the shape of
the lock. The triangle key will open the door!

Calling all clues!
Did you see the mud puddle outside the door?
Donald says that whoever took the muffins must
have stepped in the mud.

Donald checks Minnie.
There is no mud on her.
Donald checks Daisy.
There is mud on Daisy.
"You took the muffins!" he cries.
"The case is solved!"

Daisy cannot believe her ears.
She says she did not take the muffins.

Calling all clues!
Can you find something that is the same size
and shape as the muffin tray?

PUZZLES

Good work!
The puzzle box is the same size and shape as
the muffin tray.
Daisy has an idea. She puts the box down on
the table. She turns the fan on.
What happens?

Calling all clues!

Look at where the puzzle box landed.

Daisy points to the mud-covered box.

"The muffins are in there," she says, "but the lid is stuck because it's covered with mud."

Oh, Toodles!

Can you show us the Mystery Mouseketool?

PUZZLES

It's a crowbar!
Daisy uses the crowbar to open
the box.
Super cheers!
The muffins are inside, and now they are
cool enough to eat.
Come on, everybody!
It's muffin time!

Do you know the best thing about muffins?
When all your muffins are gone,
it's easy to make some more!

MICKEY'S BLUEBERRY MUFFINS

(From *Mickey's Gourmet Cookbook* © 1994 Hyperion, ISBN: 0-7868-8016-3)

YOU NEED:

3/4 cup of bread flour
3/4 cup of cake flour
1/2 cup of sugar
3/4 teaspoon of salt
2 tablespoons of dry milk powder

3 teaspoons of baking powder
1/4 cup of shortening
1/2 cup of water
2 egg whites
1/2 cup of blueberries, fresh or frozen

WHAT YOU DO:

1. Have a grown-up help you preheat the oven to 350°. Line the muffin tray cups with paper liners.
2. In a bowl, sift together flours, sugar, salt, dry milk powder, and baking powder.
3. Have a grown-up cut in shortening with a pastry cutter and blend until lumps are about the size of peas.
4. Combine water and egg whites with a fork; do not whip.
5. Add wet ingredients to dry ingredients and mix only long enough to moisten. Batter will be lumpy.
6. Spoon into paper-lined muffin cups and bake for 20 to 25 minutes, or until nicely browned.

Makes 12 muffins.

Are We There Yet?

A LEVEL 1 EARLY READER

By Sheila Sweeny Higginson

Illustrated by the Disney Storybook Artists

DISNEP PRESS

NEW YORK

Let's go to the beach!

Mickey sees one cactus.

Minnie sees two lizards.

Are we there yet?
No. This is not the beach.

SANDY
BEACH
11 MILES

RAIN FOREST
100 MILES

Donald sees three frogs.

Daisy sees four parrots.

Are we there yet?
No. This is not the beach.

SANDY
BEACH
111miles

ANTARCTICA
1000miles

Welcome
to the
RAIN FOREST

89

Goofy sees five seals.

Pluto sees six penguins.

Are we there yet?
No. This is not the beach.

Welcome to ANTARCTICA

SANDY BEACH 1111 miles

COOL FOREST 1110 miles

93

Mickey sees seven deer.

Minnie sees eight rabbits.

Are we there yet?
No. This is not the beach.

Welcome
to the
CooL FOREST

Donald sees nine starfish.

Daisy sees ten crabs.

Are we there yet?
Yes!

101

This is the beach.
Let's have fun!

OVER THE RIVER

A LEVEL 1 EARLY READER

By Sheila Sweeny Higginson
Illustrated by the Disney Storybook Artists

DISNEY PRESS

NEW YORK

Mickey got a letter.
Who sent it?

Dear  ,

Mickey

Come to our cottage

for a picnic.

Use the map.

from,

Goldilocks and
the Three Bears

105

Mickey has to follow the map. Can you help?

First, to go out of the ,
find the round door.

To go over the  river,
choose a tool.

Cheers! Mickey used the boat.
Next, go up a 🏔. hill
Find the highest one.

Hot dog! We found it!
Now, to go through the
choose a tool.

dark forest

Cheers! Mickey used the fireflies. To go across the , count the stones.

pond

Good job! There were five stones. Now, to go down the [cliff], choose a tool.

cliff

Cheers! Mickey used the rope. Next, go between the 🌲🌲🌲. Find the tallest ones.

trees

Hot dog! We're almost there! To go under the rocks, choose a tool.

Super cheers! Mickey used the shovel. Now, go into the

meadow

. Find the green one.

Hot dog! We're here! It's time to eat!

Pluto's Best

A Level Pre-1 Early Reader

By Susan Ring

Illustrated by Loter, Inc.

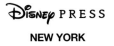
PRESS

NEW YORK

Meeska, Mooska, Mickey Mouse!

Let's go into my [hand] [Mickey] [house] .
Clubhouse

is going to be in a contest.

Pluto

 is going to be in it, too.

Butch

They both want to win the big 🏆 .

prize

131

Oh, Toodles!

Here are today's Mousketools:

five yellow  , a ⊙ , and a ⟋ .

balls   life preserver   whistle

Goofy begins the contest.

Oh, no!  only has one .
ball

Pluto

He needs to juggle six .
balls

Oh, Toodles!

Do you see a tool that could help Pluto?

Yes! can use the five yellow .

Pluto   balls

134

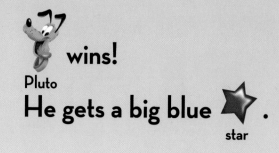 wins!

Pluto

He gets a big blue ⭐.

star

Pluto and Butch run and jump.

Oh, no! Pluto, come back!

Pluto can't hear us.

Oh, Toodles!

Which tool can we use to call Pluto ?

Cheers! We'll use the whistle .

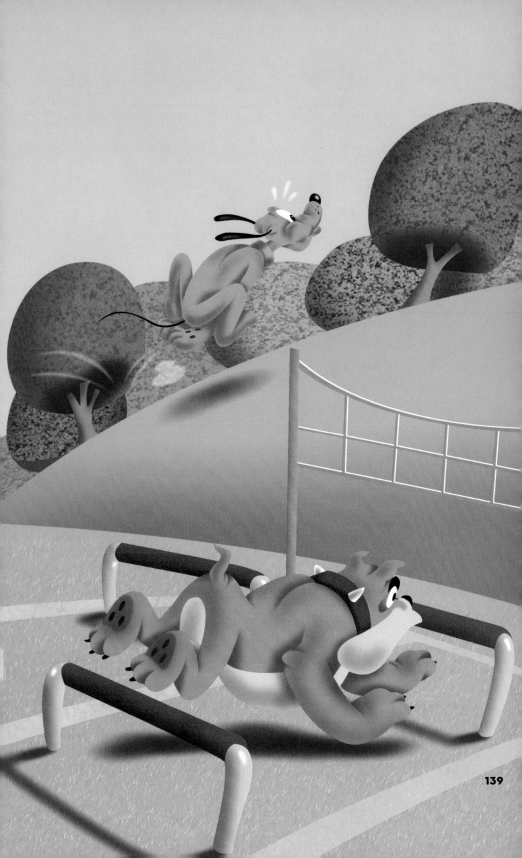

Butch  wins!

He gets a big red ⭐ .

star

Butch wins the next game—wagon pulling.
He has two stars.
How many does Pluto have?

142

Now it is time to swim.

Who will get to the end of the pool first?

Oh, no! Butch needs help.

Oh, Toodles!

Will the life preserver help save Butch?

Yes!

Go,  , go!

Pluto

You can help  .

Butch

 helps  get to the end!

Pluto   Butch

146

 wins!

Butch

He gets a big red  .

star

He gives it to  .

Pluto

148

Now  and  have the same number

Butch   Pluto

of  .

stars

Let's count them!

Yes, they have two  each.

stars

They both share the big  !

prize

150

Mickey's Campout

A Level Pre-1 Early Reader

By Susan Ring

Illustrated by Loter, Inc.

Ðisnep PRESS

NEW YORK

Hi, everybody!

Can you say Meeska, Mooska,

Mickey Mouse?

Let's go to the  Clubhouse !

We are going camping.

First we will set up a tent.

Then we will have a  .

campfire

Toodles has our Mouseketools.

They are a pot , a woodpecker , and a ? .

pot   woodpecker   Mystery
                                            Mousketool

We are all here!

Minnie, Daisy, Donald, Pluto, Goofy,

and Pete are going camping, too.

Is everybody ready?

Don't forget the tents.

Camping is fun!

Let's set up the first  .
tent

This tent is for Mickey and Donald .

Uh-oh. The tent is not right.

The pole is too long.

How can we make it shorter?

159

Mickey can't fix the  .
tent

Donald can't fix the tent.

Can anyone fix the tent?

We must cut the ⟋ .
pole

Oh, !
Toodles

Which tool should we use?

160

That's right!

The  ! He can cut the _____ .

woodpecker   pole

Now, Donald and Mickey can set up

their _____ .

tent

and tried to set up their tent.

Daisy   Minnie

The tent should look like a big .

balloon

But it is flat like a .

plate

Daisy can't fix the tent.

Minnie can't fix the tent.

Who can fix the tent?

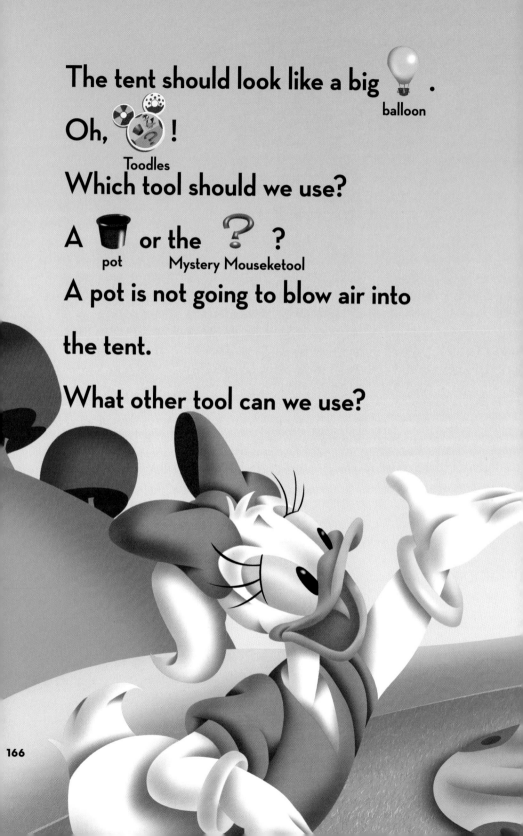

The tent should look like a big .

balloon

Oh, !

Toodles

Which tool should we use?

A or the ?

pot   Mystery Mouseketool

A pot is not going to blow air into

the tent.

What other tool can we use?

That's right! The  ? is a ⚡.

Mystery Mouseketool   fan

It will blow air into the tent.

It will make the tent look like a big 🎈.

balloon

Now, 🦆 and 🐭 can set up their

Daisy   Minnie

tent.

168

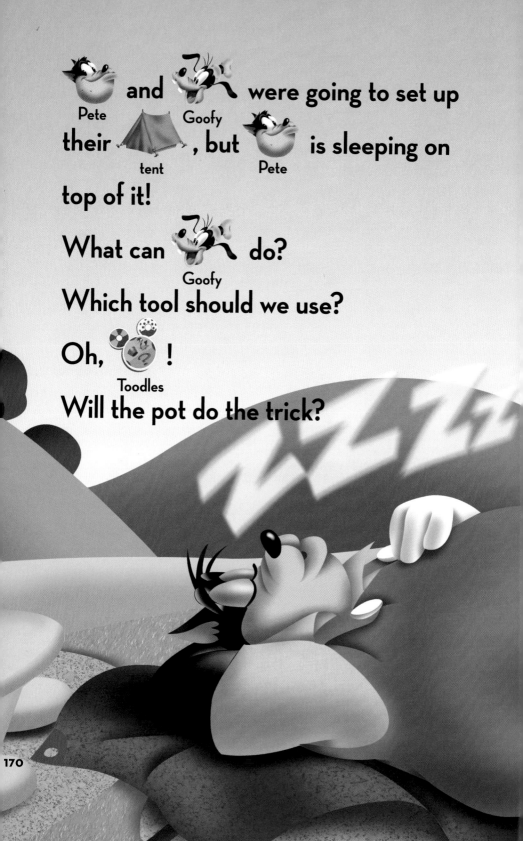

 and were going to set up
Pete   Goofy

their , but is sleeping on
            tent   Pete

top of it!

What can do?
              Goofy

Which tool should we use?

Oh, !
      Toodles

Will the pot do the trick?

170

171

Yes! The  pot is the right tool for  Goofy!

 Pete wakes up!

Now  Goofy and  Pete can set up their  tent.

All of the ![tents] are up.

tents

Mickey and Donald make a ![campfire] .

campfire

Minnie has a special treat.

It is one of the best things about

camping: ![marshmallows] !

marshmallows